JP

The Magician and McTree

by Patricia Coombs

Lothrop, Lee & Shepard Books
New York

First Edition   1   2   3   4   5   6   7   8   9   10

Library of Congress Cataloging in Publication Data
Coombs, Patricia. The magician and McTree.
Summary: By mistake an old, old magician causes his cat McTree to talk, and thus begins a series of exciting adventures for the feline.
[1. Cats—Fiction.   2. Magicians—Fiction]   I. Title.
PZ7.C7813Mag   1984   [E]   83-11984
ISBN 0-688-02109-3   ISBN 0-688-02111-5 (lib. bdg.)

ONCE UPON A TIME,

long, long ago, there was a cat. His name was McTree. He lived with an old, old magician in a small hut in a big forest.

One day the old, old magician got out his cauldron. He began mixing up a potion. It was cough medicine. He made it every year to sell in the village beyond the forest. McTree sat among the pots and bottles and watched.

Part way through the recipe, the old, old magician forgot what he was doing. He threw in some mint, a cobweb, a clothespin, and two toadstools. He mumbled and scratched his head. A moth flew out of his hat.

With a wild leap, McTree made a grab for the moth. He missed. With a splash, he fell into the cauldron. When he climbed out, McTree found that he was able to talk.

"A towel, quick!" said McTree.

"Oh, oh, trouble!" said the old, old magician as he dried McTree's wet fur.

"Ouch!" said McTree. "Easy around those ears!"

"McTree," said the old, old magician, "don't ever let *anybody* know that you can talk. Keep it to yourself, or you will get into a lot of trouble. And you will get me into even *more* trouble."

McTree nodded. "Right," said McTree. "I'll keep it quiet. My lips are sealed."

The old, old magician sighed. He went back to stirring the potion. He added some raspberry jam, a button, and a cup of tea he had forgotten to drink.

Days went by. McTree badly wanted to talk to travelers passing the hut, but he didn't. He longed to tell them stories. But he didn't. He spoke only to the old, old magician. And when he went for walks in the forest, McTree talked to himself and sang.

"Tum ti ti tum," warbled McTree as he strolled along under the trees.

One day, walking along, McTree stopped by a pool. He saw himself in the water.

"Ah," murmured McTree, "what a handsome cat I am. A pity that people do not know about me. I would be famous. My picture would be on posters in the villages . . ." McTree was so busy daydreaming that he walked right into the bog.

"Help! Help!" cried McTree.

An old woman was in the forest. She was digging truffles with her white truffle pig. She couldn't see very well, the pig having stepped on her glasses, but she heard McTree's cries. She hurried to the bog and peered around.

"Over here! Over here!" cried McTree.

"It must be a small child," muttered the old woman. "Perhaps with rich parents. I will get a reward!" She took a long stick and pushed it out into the bog. McTree climbed on. The old woman pulled. With much huffing and puffing she pulled McTree from the bog.

"Many thanks, old woman," said McTree. McTree rolled himself in leaves and grass to clean the mud from his fur, talking all the while.

When the old woman saw that it was a cat and not a child she'd saved, and that the cat was talking to her, she threw herself on the ground.

"*Aaaaaaiiiiii!*" she wailed. "A spell has been cast on me, *aaaaaaaiiiiiii!*"

"Do be quiet," said McTree. "Nobody has cast a spell on you. You're all right. Let me help you up. McTree is the name."

At last the old woman grew quiet. McTree talked and talked. He made up adventures he'd never had. The old woman listened, amazed.

Suddenly she let out a cry. She looked around. "My pig! My pig! My basket of truffles!"

"Your pig is asleep over by that tree," said McTree. "I fear he has eaten the truffles."

"*Aaaaaiiii!*" cried the old woman. "Whatever shall I do? I must have truffles for the King's dinner party. Oh . . . ahhh." A light glinted in the old woman's eyes.

As McTree opened his mouth to sing a song for her, the old woman grabbed him. She wrapped him up in her apron and stuffed him into the truffle basket.

The old woman chuckled as she made her way toward the castle.

"*Help, help, help!*" screamed McTree, fighting to get out of the basket.

"Save your breath, McTree," snapped the old woman. "You're about to be given away. And I'm about to be rich!"

McTree groaned. The truffle pig grunted. The old woman puffed and chuckled as she climbed the castle steps. A guard stood beside the castle door.

"Get me out of here!" screamed McTree.

The guard jumped. "Noisy truffles you've got, old woman."

"A special present for the King," said the old woman.

"A special present, eh? All right. This way," said the guard.

"I've been kidnapped!" howled McTree. "Let me out!"

"Do shush," hissed the old woman. "You'll do us all in with that great mouth of yours, McTree."

The King looked up from his dinner. He saw the old woman, a pig, and a basket that howled and jerked. The King frowned and got to his feet.

"What are you doing in the royal dining room?" cried the King. "You're too late with my truffles. Guard, take that old crone to the dungeon. Take that pig to the kitchen and roast it."

"Now, now," said the Queen. "Remember your ulcer. Sit down and be quiet."

"Your Majesty," said the old woman, "instead of truffles I have brought you a priceless gift. It is a famous talking cat."

"Hmph!" said the King, eyeing the basket. "If it is famous, why have I not heard of it? If I have not heard of it, it isn't famous."

The old woman shuffled and bobbed. "I was teaching him speech fit for a king. Months I have worked . . ."

"*Liar!*" screamed McTree, thinking fast. "This old witch turned me into a cat!"

With that, the old woman dropped the basket, grabbed McTree by the neck, and began to choke him.

"*Aaarrgggh!*" gasped McTree.

The guard grabbed the old woman. McTree rolled from her grasp and put his paws to his throat.

"*Ahem. Do re mi. La, la, la, la!*" sang McTree. He bowed. "Thank goodness my voice was not harmed by that brutal attack," said he.

The King, the Queen, and all the guests sat with their mouths open.

"It *is* a cat," said the Queen.

"And it *does* talk," said the King.

"And sing!" said the Queen. "Just think, duets with the royal canaries. I'll be the envy of everyone!"

"Let me go, let me go!" cried the old woman.

"As a favor to me, let her go," said McTree. "She did save my life."

The Queen gave the old woman a handful of silver. "Run along," said the Queen, "and take the pig with you."

The old woman and the pig scurried out of the castle.

"Ah, that was a close one," said McTree. "Though it hardly compares with my fight with Black Jack the pirate off the coast of France."

"Do tell us!" said the Queen. "But first, some dinner." She had a place set for McTree beside her at the table. The servants brought bowls of cream, and fish fillets on a silver dish.

Having eaten his fill, McTree began to talk. He talked and talked. He made up all kinds of adventures. The King, the Queen, and all the guests *oh*'d and *ah*'d. Their eyes grew round. They gasped. They clapped.

News of the talking cat spread all over the kingdom. Soon the roads to the castle were crowded. People waited in line for hours to hear McTree talk and sing songs. Everyone envied the King and Queen their famous talking cat.

McTree was allowed to sit on the King's throne. He had velvet pillows to sleep on. He was given the best of food. He had a solid gold litter box with his name on it. The Queen gave him toys and tidbits.

Every night the king came to hear McTree tell a bedtime story.

Sometimes, after the crowds had left, McTree would think about the old, old magician. He'd remember his own promise. McTree would feel pangs. He would squeeze his eyes shut and go to sleep.

As time went on, McTree grew spoiled and fat from living at the castle. He forgot about the old, old magician and the little hut in the forest.

But, as usually happens with most novelties, people began to grow bored with McTree. Fewer and fewer of them came to see him. The Queen didn't bring him tidbits anymore. The King was tired of his stories. McTree talked less and less. He slept more and more.

One day, between yawns, The Queen said to the King, "If our kingdom is to be famous for its wonders, one fat, lazy braggart of a cat will not do. We have had only six visitors this week. They were *nobodies*. We need *more* talking animals."

"Hmmm," said the King, "that cat once said something about an old magician. Call the guards. Have the magician brought to me at once."

Meanwhile, on the other side of the kingdom, a Princess heard someone talking about McTree. "Aha," said the Princess to herself, "it cannot *really* be a cat. Underneath there is a handsome Prince. I will save him. One kiss and he will be mine. We will live happily ever after."

The Princess called for her tailor and seamstress. She ordered a pair of stout leather gloves and an enormous fur muff. She ordered a small satin tunic with ruffles. Then she ordered a large yellow cat to be brought in secretly from the stables.

A few days later, the Princess climbed the steps to the castle. The King and Queen showed her into McTree's special room. McTree was sitting on a velvet cushion, yawning at a catnip mouse.

"Leave me alone with him," said the Princess. "I have heard that he is a fake, a fraud."

"Well, really!" said the Queen, walking off in a huff.

"The nerve!" said the King, slamming the door.

Quick as a flash, the Princess put the stable cat on the pillows. She stuffed McTree into her fur muff.

"What are you doing?" screamed McTree.

"Hush, sweetheart," whispered the Princess. "I am here to save you. You will soon be your own handsome self again, do not fear."

"What are you, crazy?" cried McTree. "I already *am* my own handsome self." McTree tried to bite the Princess, but his teeth got stuck in her leather glove.

Out of the castle and down the steps swept the Princess. "Your cat is a fake!" she cried to the King and Queen as she leaped into her carriage.

She took McTree out of her muff. She unhooked his teeth from her glove.

"There you are, mudjums lovey," crooned the Princess as McTree glared and snarled. "Now we'll see how booful you look all dressed up." With that, the Princess stuffed McTree into the little white satin tunic.

Just then there was a shout. The carriage rattled to a stop. The door was flung open. It was a bandit.

"Your gold and jewels!" he shouted. McTree shot off the Princess's lap and scrambled on top of the carriage.

The Princess yelled at the bandit. "You fool! You let the cat out! Get him, get him!" She began pounding on the bandit with her stout leather gloves. She knocked him over and gave him a black eye. She jumped out of the carriage to hit him again.

McTree quickly jumped on top of the horse. "Giddyap!" cried McTree. And off shot the carriage down the road.

"I'm going home. Back to the simple life. Back to my wise old friend," said McTree. On and on he galloped, down the road and through the village.

The old truffle woman was just closing her shutters as McTree went past. She squinted and gasped.

"A fairy! An enchanted coach! I must go tell the King. I'll get a reward!" cried the old woman.

Through the forest galloped McTree. At last he saw the little hut shining in the moonlight. McTree jumped down. Blinded by tears, McTree raced inside. With a sob he leaped into the old, old magician's lap. Alas, the lap was gone. He sat alone in an empty chair.

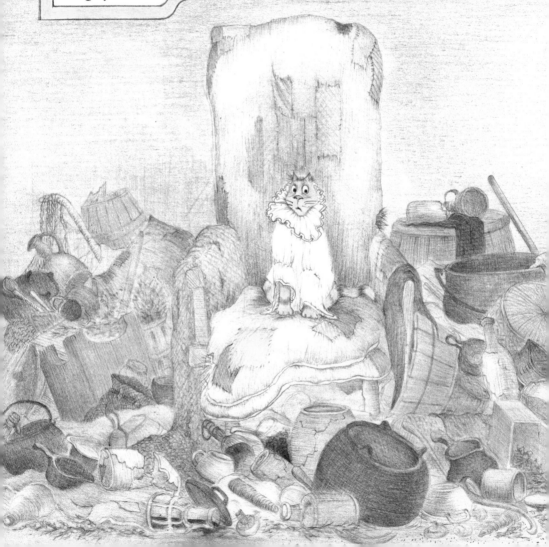

McTree blinked. He looked around. The books and potions were gone. A stool was overturned, jars and bottles were broken. There were signs of struggle everywhere.

"Foul play!" gasped McTree. "Someone has kidnapped my dear old magician. And from the looks of that glove over in the corner, the King's Guards have been here. To the rescue, McTree!" And he leaped back on the horse and galloped back through the forest, back through the village, and up the road to the castle.

At that moment, the King was shoving the old, old magician into a room with all his books and potions. The Queen came in with seven cats, five dogs, three canaries, and a fish in a bowl.

"Do the fish first," said the Queen. "I want a talking fish most of all. And this time make sure it *lasts*. That first cat, McTree, ran down. He talked less and less. Now he can't say a word."

The old, old magician wrung his hands. "But Your Majesties, I have told you the truth. That potion was a mistake. I do not know what went into it."

"Get to work! Have these animals talking by dawn, or into the dungeon you go. And no one *ever* leaves the dungeon."

With that, the King and Queen slammed the door and locked it. Off to bed they went.

McTree jumped from the horse. He sneaked through the bushes to the back door of the castle. A maid and a footman were talking by the window.

"They've got that poor old magician locked up now," said the footman.

"Yes, and the Queen, she took him all the cats and dogs, even her pet fish and the canaries. Soon they'll all be talking, so . . ."

"*What!*" cried McTree.

"*Hssst!* Someone spying on us!" said the maid. "I'll meet you in the rose garden later."

"*Other* animals? Good heavens! Dogs! A fish? I have come in the nick of time," murmured McTree.

He raced around the castle. He saw a lighted tower window. He heard the distant barking and yowling of cats and dogs.

"Aha," said McTree, "that must be where they have locked up my old friend." Up a tree and out on a limb over the fish pond went McTree. A bold leap took him to the balcony. Another leap, and he scrambled up an ivy vine. Paw over paw, higher and higher he climbed. Panting, he got his paws over the windowsill and pulled himself up. One jump, and he was inside the castle.

He looked around. "Hmmm, the upper hall. I hear the dogs down that way," murmured McTree. "Oh, oh, a guard."

McTree stayed in the shadows along the wall. He hid behind a velvet curtain.

"Pssst!" whispered McTree.

"Whaaa—?" mumbled the guard, half asleep.

"Run along," whispered McTree. "I'll stand guard for you. The maid is waiting for you in the rose garden."

"She *is*? Thanks, my friend," said the guard. He sped down the hall and around the corner, and was gone.

McTree stepped from behind the curtain. He looked at the door. The key was in the lock. With a leap and a swipe of his paw, McTree knocked the key to the floor. One more swipe and the key slid under the door.

"*Pssst*, old friend," said McTree, "the key is under the door. Hurry up."

The old, old magician shuffled to the door at the sound of McTree's voice. He unlocked it with shaking hands. McTree jumped into his arms with a wild purr, knocking him over.

"You must run, quickly!" said McTree. "We haven't much time."

"I'm too old to run!" cried the old, old magician. "It's no use, McTree. I cannot get away. And I cannot remember what was in that potion."

"Listen," said McTree, "all you have to do is mix up something strong and smelly and smokey. Get it going well, with *lots* of smoke. Then go down the hall. Turn left at the bottom of the stairs, another left, a right, and out that door. A carriage is waiting for you. Go home, and leave the rest to me."

The old, old magician poured all the bottles and jars into the cauldron. "This will have to be stirred," he said.

"I'll stir while you get out of the castle," said McTree.

Soon thick smoke and sparks and fumes began rising from the cauldron. The smoke got blacker and thicker and smellier.

"I'll take over now," whispered McTree. "Hurry, old friend. And be careful."

As McTree stirred, the old, old magician shuffled off down the hall. Great black clouds billowed and swelled around him.

McTree stirred and stirred until the smoke was so thick he could hardly breathe. Then he leaped into the hall, yelling, "Fire, fire!"

All over the castle people jumped out of their beds. They yelled. They ran up the stairs and down again. Someone cried out, "There is no fire! It's a trick!"

The King and Queen raced up the stairs. "He's gone!" yelled the King. "The magician has escaped!"

"Hurry!" screamed the Queen. "We must get him. I'll have my talking fish or that magician's head!"

The King called out his two squadrons of knights. "You go that way," said the King. "The Queen and I will ride with the others. A fat reward awaits whoever finds the magician and brings him to me!" Off into the night they galloped.

McTree dashed ahead of them. "This way, this way!" called McTree. "Over here, over here!" he hallooed.

An hour passed, and then another, as McTree led them in circles deeper and deeper into the forest.

When he got to the bog, McTree scrambled out on a limb. *"Here! Right here! Quickly! Full gallop!"* he shouted.

Full speed, the King and the Queen and all the knights galloped right into the bog and began to sink.

"Help, help!" they all cried.

The old truffle woman came trudging along. She squinted at the bog and scowled. "The whole bog is full of talking cats now. I'll not help *them*." And off she went toward the castle.

The Queen was screaming at the King. "Get me out of here at once!"

"It's your fault we're in this mess," snapped the King. "You and your talking fish!"

"It's better than talking to you!" cried the Queen.

"Be quiet and listen to me," said McTree in his deepest, meanest voice. "If you want to get out of the bog alive, you must leave the old magician alone. If you don't, worse things than this bog will befall you."

"I promise, I promise," cried the Queen.

"I promise, I promise," cried the King. "Just get us out of here. I never want to see another magician!"

McTree sped off into the forest, hallooing for the other squadron of knights. They came galloping to the rescue.

Tired, but not too tired to sing a marching song, McTree padded off down the path that led back to the little hut. The old, old magician was waiting for him with a bowl of warm milk and a good fire.

"McTree," said the old, old magician, "you really *are* a hero!"

McTree rubbed against the old, old magician. He didn't say a word. He just sat in his friend's lap and purred until they both fell asleep.